THOMAS & FRIENDS™

BUMPER BOOK!

THOMAS & FRIENDS™

EGMONT
We bring stories to life

First published in Great Britain in 2014
This edition published in 2017 by Dean,
an imprint of Egmont UK Limited,
The Yellow Building
1 Nicholas Road
London W11 4AN

HiT entertainment

Thomas the Tank Engine & Friends™

ISBN 978 0 6035 6962 3
58215/3
Printed in the EU

Let's Colour

What is The Fat Controller holding in his hand? Join the dots to find out. Then add some colour to the rainbow and the rest of the picture.

MAVIS

THE FFARQUHAR QUARRY CO.LTD.

Look at the picture below.
Can you answer the questions in the boxes?

How many birds can you spot?

How many hats can you count?

How many stars can you see?

RHENEAS

2

Write over the number in the box.

Let's Colour!

Flora is the only girl tram engine on the island of Sodor!

1

Colour in Flora with **yellow** and **red** pencils.

SODOR TRAMWAYS

Flora

Here's a picture of Flora to help you colour her in.

Thomas was worried that Toby wouldn't want another tram engine on Sodor but when he met Flora, Toby liked her a lot.

2

Flora is yellow and red. **Colour** in each word with the right colour.

red

yellow

3

Try saying "Red lorry, yellow lolly, red lolly, yellow lorry" over and over as fast as you can. What happens?

red lorry

yellow lolly

red lolly   **yellow lorry**

1 Can you **find** these things in the big picture? Tick the box when you find each one.

2 Which engine is steaming past the playing fields?

James

Let's look at faces!

Look in a mirror. What faces can you make? Can you look surprised?

1 Look at Gordon and the carriage. Which one do you think looks cross? Write over the word.

cross

3 How do you think Thomas is feeling in each of these pictures?

a

b

Looking at faces can tell you how someone is feeling. Smiling usually means they are happy. Look at all the faces on these pages.

2

Look at Gordon and Percy. Which one do you think looks happy? Write over the word.

How many faces can you count on the page?

happy

c

d

Let's read!

One cold and frosty morning 's Fireman couldn't get to the Yard. The roads were too  so  had to roll up his sleeves and get  ready for work.  made sure that 's firebox was nice and clean and ready for new . It was a messy job and  was soon covered in  dust. He put fresh  in the firebox and started the engine's fire so  could get up steam. "I can't spend all day covered in  dust,"  said, "I'll have to go home to change my clothes." But  was worried about the  roads. Train

Special key

Duck   **icy**   **The Fat Controller**   **coal**

tracks passed by 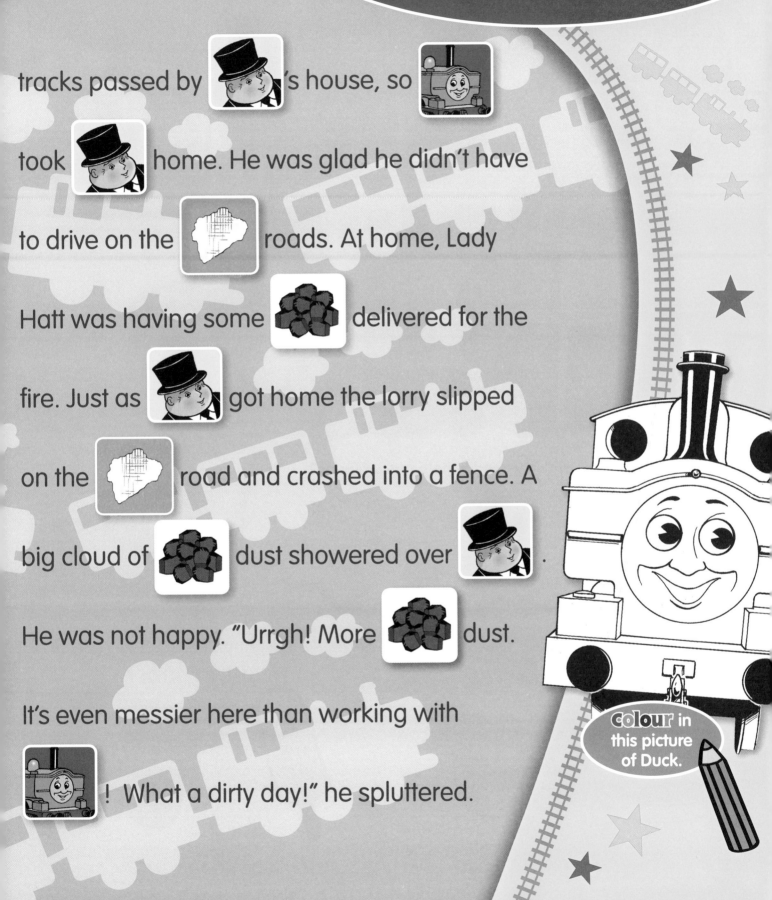's house, so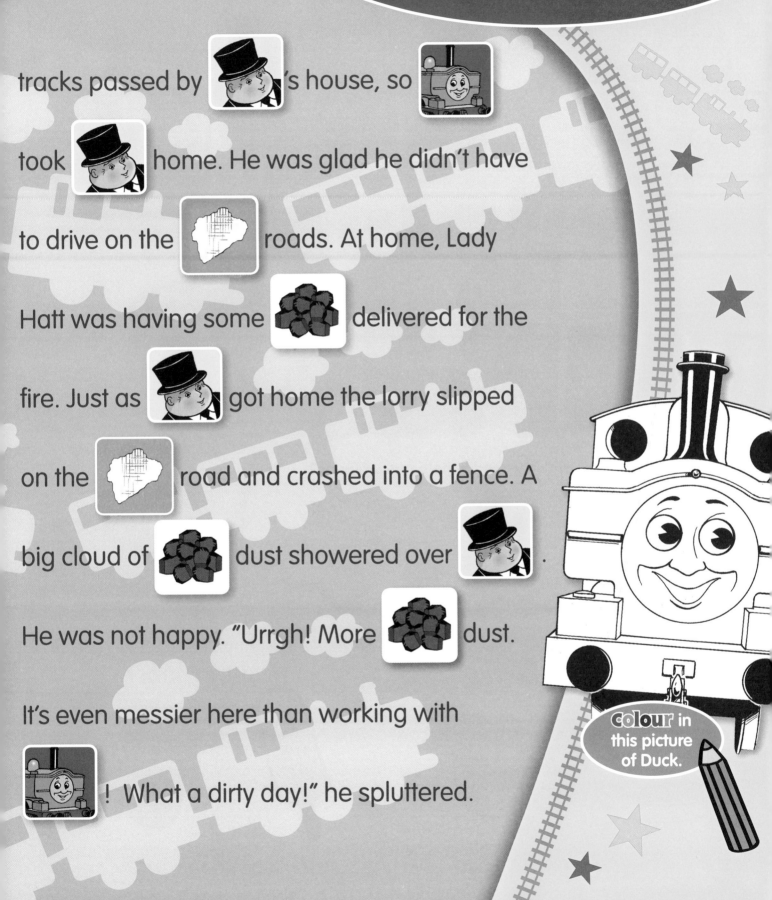

took home. He was glad he didn't have

to drive on the roads. At home, Lady

Hatt was having some delivered for the

fire. Just as got home the lorry slipped

on the road and crashed into a fence. A

big cloud of dust showered over .

He was not happy. "Urrgh! More dust.

It's even messier here than working with

! What a dirty day!" he spluttered.

Colour in this picture of Duck.

Let's get puzzling!

This puzzle page is all about food and fuel.

1 Chocolate won't make you go, Percy! Can you find the missing piece from this funny picture?

a

b

c

What does Percy need to help make him go?

fuel

2 There are two healthy snacks and two special treats. Can you circle the two healthy foods?

What colour are cherries and strawberries?

Let's Colour

Coloured by:

1

Thomas

 Thomas is a cheeky, fussy little engine. He often gets into trouble with best friend, Percy.

Thomas likes to do big important jobs even when he hasn't done them before. It often leads to all sorts of problems!

Thomas always fixes his mistakes and The Fat Controller thinks Thomas is Really Useful. That's why Thomas was given his own branch line!

When **Emily** first came to the Island of Sodor, she took Thomas' carriages by mistake!

2 **colour** in Annie with an **orange** pencil.

Use this picture of **Emily** and **Annie** as a colour guide.

Duck is called Duck because all the engines think he waddles!

1

The geese wouldn't budge so he became cross. "They'll make me late!" grumbled Duck. His Driver and Guard shooed the geese away.

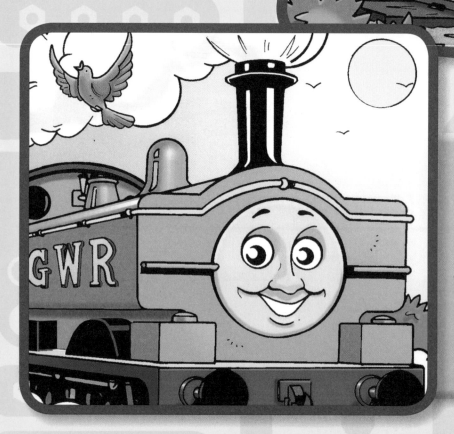

2

One morning, Duck was happily puffing along his branch line. The sun was shining and the birds were tweeting.

This story has been all jumbled up. Read the story then write the numbers in the right order below.

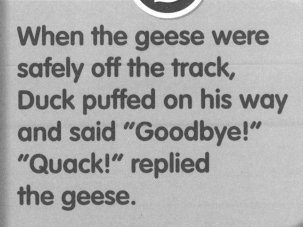

3

When the geese were safely off the track, Duck puffed on his way and said "Goodbye!" "Quack!" replied the geese.

4

Just then, Duck spotted some geese that had waddled onto the track. "You shouldn't be here!" he smiled.

The right order is:

Let's Colour!

S C C

BILL

BRENDAM BAY

We like teasing other engines...

Draw over the line to follow the path of the falling rocks.

Did you know?

Bill and Ben once saved all the Quarry workers when there was a rockslide.

Apart from their nameplates, Bill and Ben are identical in every way. **colour** in Ben using Bill as a guide.

BRENDAM BAY

S C C

BEN

...and getting up to all sorts of mischief!

Draw some more rocks. Then **colour** in the Workman.

Let's get going!

START

1 Write over the word below and when you are ready, shout "Go!"

go

2 It's time to pick up the parcel. Draw over the dotted lines and then help load it onto Thomas.

Wave the green flag like a guard!

4 Thomas stops for a drink. Pretend you are Thomas at the water tower. What noises would you make?

Thomas needs to be a Really Useful engine and make a special delivery. Help him to get his wheels whizzing so he can deliver his parcel in super quick time.

The Fat Controller

3

Cinders and ashes! There is a signal ahead! Write over the word while Thomas waits.

stop

Splendid work, Thomas!

FINISH

5

Draw a picture of a station for Thomas to pull into when he arrives.

Let's read!

Harvey finds a new job when Thomas has to advertise his ride!

One day  was delivering  to the Docks. He saw an aeroplane pulling a big  across the sky.

"See Sodor by Air!" it read. "People should see it by rail too!" thought . He was so busy looking up he didn't spot some oil on the track and skidded off. The  went everywhere!  the Crane Engine was sent to get  back on the track and the  back into the trucks. While  worked he told  of all the things he had lifted with his hook. "There's nothing you haven't hooked!" smiled  as he headed off to deliver the  at last. Then The Fat Controller told  he would be

Special key

banner   crates   Harvey   Thomas

taking a Sodor Special tourist train.

"No more 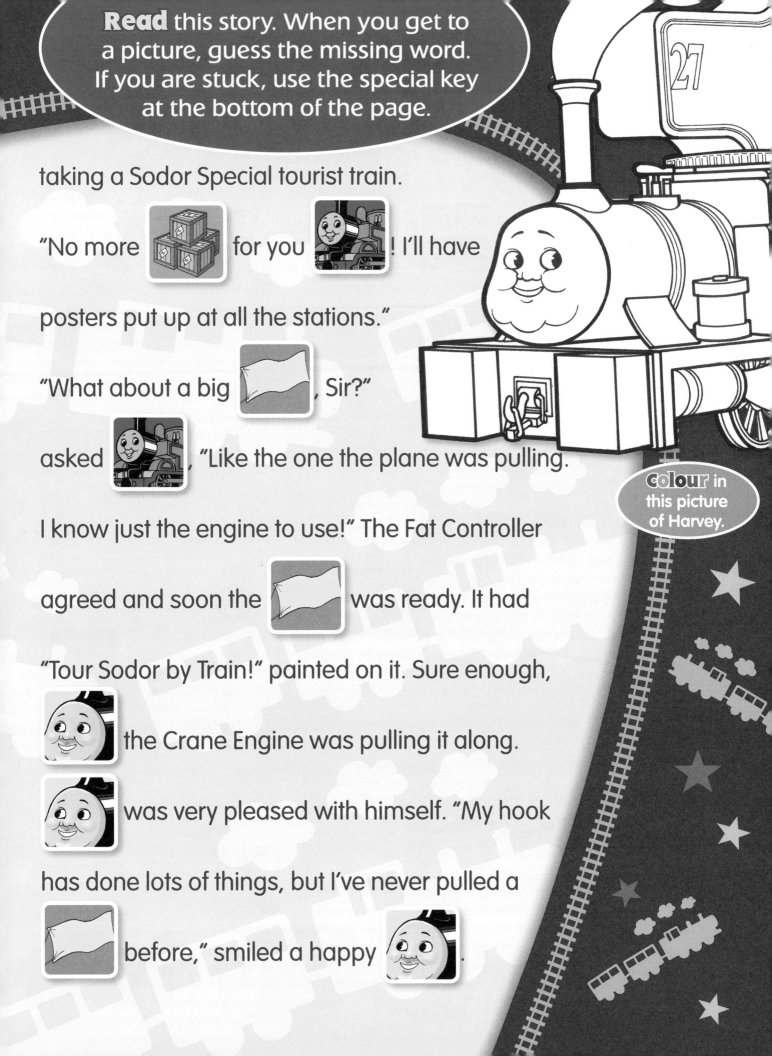 for you 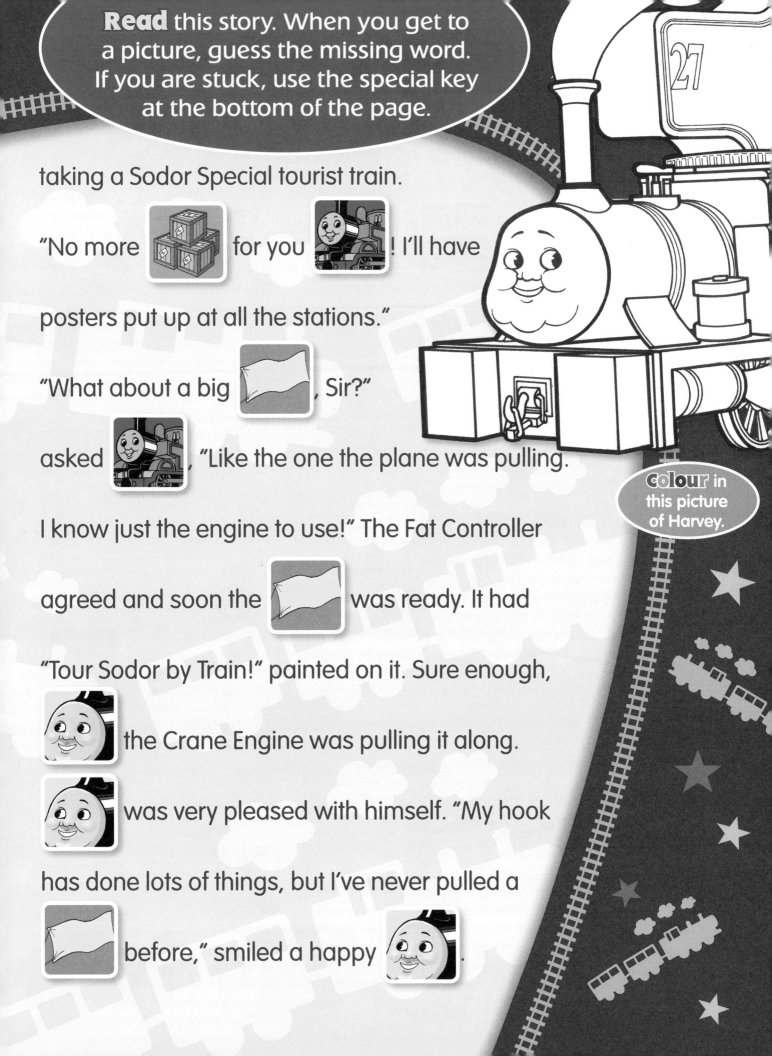! I'll have

posters put up at all the stations."

"What about a big 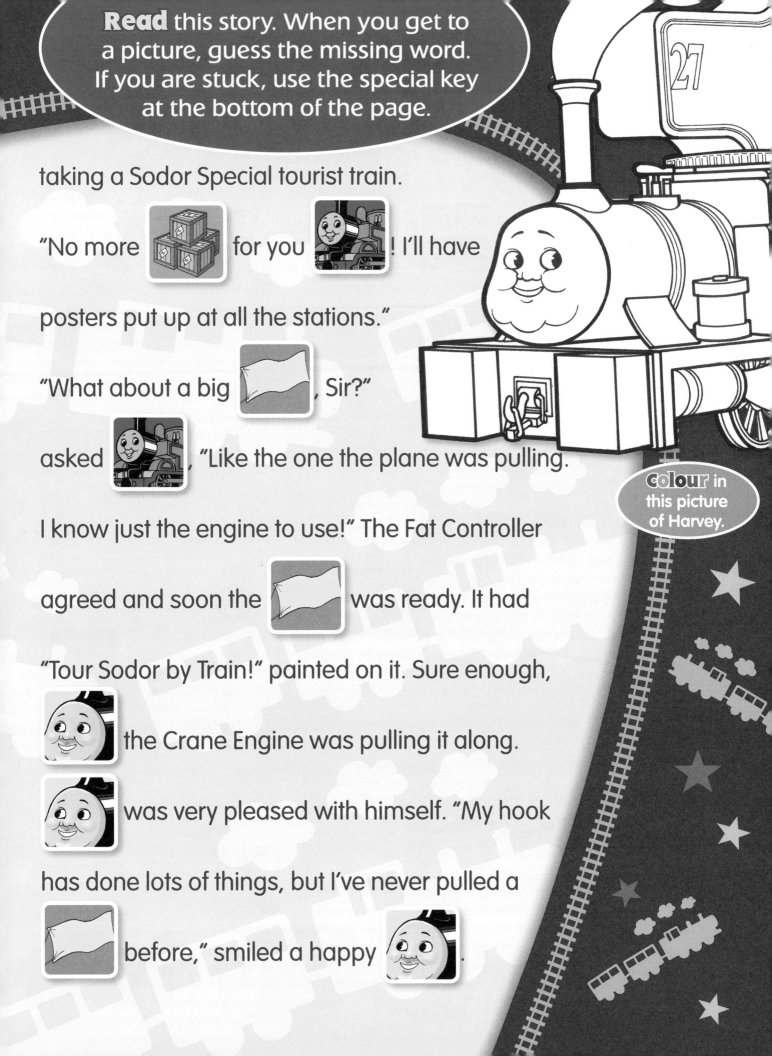, Sir?"

asked , "Like the one the plane was pulling.

I know just the engine to use!" The Fat Controller

agreed and soon the was ready. It had

"Tour Sodor by Train!" painted on it. Sure enough,

 the Crane Engine was pulling it along.

 was very pleased with himself. "My hook

has done lots of things, but I've never pulled a

 before," smiled a happy .

Colour in this picture of Harvey.

Let's get puzzling!

This puzzle page is all about **hot** and **cold**.

1

It's a hot day at the beach. Everyone is eating ice cream to cool down. Which piece is missing from the picture?

a

b

c

What should people drink when they are hot?

water

2

Look at these hot coals. Circle the largest coals.

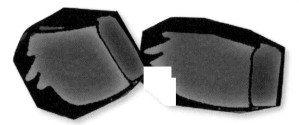

3

Can you tick the cold objects from these pairs?

4

Percy is feeling overheated! Take his steaming temperature and write the number in the box.

Bust my buffers, I feel terrible!

— 40

— 30

— 20

— 10

— 0

Percy's temperature is [ ] °C

Here's **Jack**, a hard-working, friendly front loader with a scoop. He's always lifting and clearing, helping to build roads!

3 The windmill has just been built and needs a coat of paint. Can you give it a splash of colour?

Use this picture of **Jack** as a colour guide.

2 Draw a huge heap of big rocks for Jack to scoop!

Draw a line between each funny fish and its shadow.

How many fish have the children spotted in the river?

Draw over the lines so The Fat Controller can carry on down the river.

Answers: 1. Toby is number 7. There are 8 people, 4 sponges, 2 buckets and 4 birds.

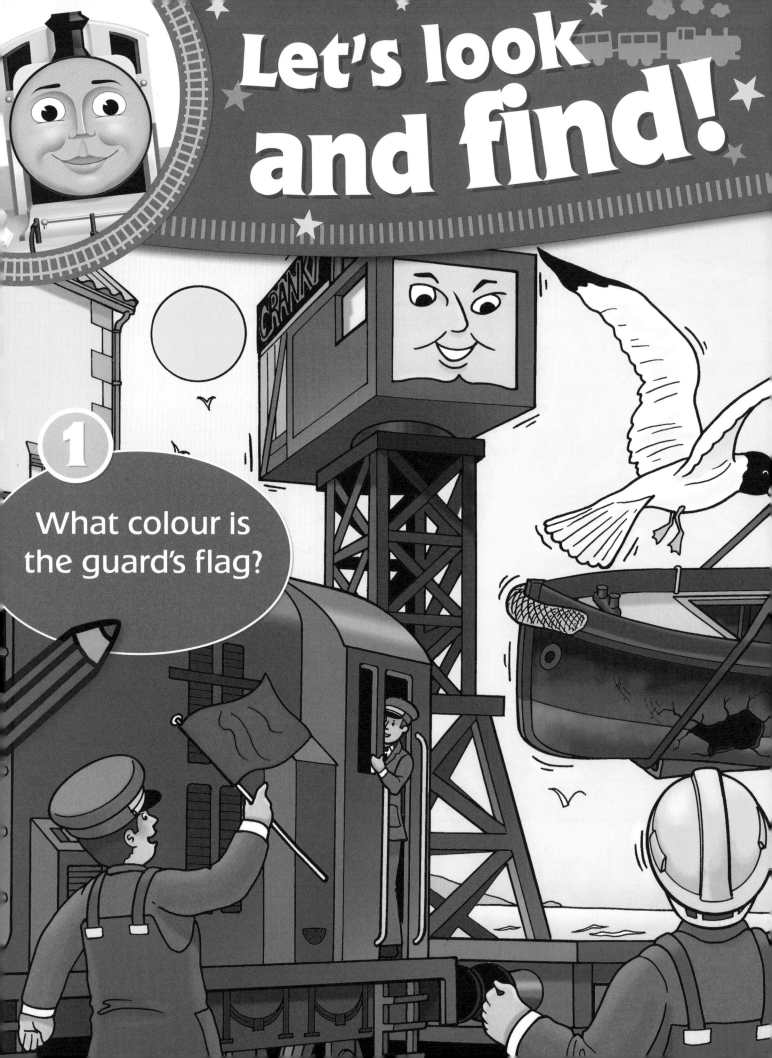

Counting Corner

How many people are moving parcels in the big picture?

Look at this row of parcels. Which is the odd one out?

This label has come off the parcel. Who is it for? Trace over the letters to find out.

Thomas

Now draw a big postage stamp for the parcel.

Here are some more parcels. How many are there?

Let's lift loads!

Have you ever lifted something that was very, very heavy? What was it?

1 Look at Harvey. What is he lifting? Write over the word.

logs

2 Here are three crates for Harvey to lift. Which one do you think is the lightest?

a coal

b leaves

c sand

There are always loads to be lifted on The Island of Sodor. Harvey and Cranky are always busy.

3 What does Cranky have at the end of his arm to lift heavy loads? Draw over the dots to find out.

hook

CRANKY

4 How many loads can you count on the page?

The lightest load is

Let's read!

Both Bertie and Thomas have to wait at signs and signals!

"Where is ? He's late," grumbled Thomas

They usually met at the station where the passengers changed.

"We can't wait for him any longer," said the Guard, "we've got a

green ." He was ready to send on his way, but

 didn't want to leave the passengers. Just then,

heard a horn tooting and rumbled into view. He raced

down the road to the station. "Sorry I'm late," gasped , "I

was stuck for ages at some new ." Thomas scoffed. "Huh!

Engines never have to worry about !" With the passengers

finally on board, the Guard waved his flag and hurried

Read this story. When you get to a picture, guess the missing word. If you are stuck use the special key on the right of the page.

away. Soon he came to a junction.

A  that was usually up so that

 could go, was against him.

"Bother that !" fumed  as he stopped.

Then while  waited, he understood how

 had felt at the . When the

went up,  sped away. He puffed

extra hard and arrived at the Main Station

a minute early. But he never teased

about  again. Now he knew where

roads have , railways have a !

Colour in this picture of Bertie.

Special key

Bertie

Thomas

signal

traffic lights

Let's get puzzling!

This puzzle page is all about friends.

1

Percy and Thomas are best friends! Can you find the missing piece from this picture?

a

b

c

Use a pencil to practise writing the word 'friends'.

friends

2

The engines are playing hide and peep. Skarloey wants to find his friend Rheneas. Circle the bush he is hiding behind.

Rheneas is red like me!

a

b

c

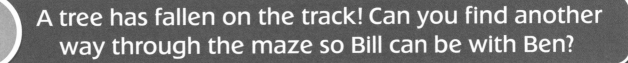

3

A tree has fallen on the track! Can you find another way through the maze so Bill can be with Ben?

Toot Toot

4

Thomas asked The Fat Controller for a surprise party for his best friend Percy. Look at the picture then complete the sum.

Happy Birthday Percy!

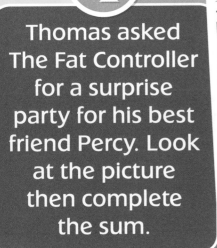

People **+** Engines **=** Altogether

James

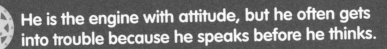

James is the only red engine in the Steam Team. This makes him very proud and he is never dull!

He is the engine with attitude, but he often gets into trouble because he speaks before he thinks.

He is an all-purpose engine and works on the main and branch lines. He can pull trucks and coaches.

Let's colour

Harold has spotted some fellow flyers. What are they? Colour in the dotted shapes to find out. Then add some colour to the rest of the picture.

HAROLD

Here's Spencer, a splendid **silver** steam engine! He thinks he is very special because he is owned by a Duke and Duchess.

Lots of things are a **silver** colour, but not all of them are precious! Look at these pictures then write over the words.

bin

bucket

spoon

Draw over these **silver** coins and then colour them in!

Look at the picture below.
Can you answer the questions
in the boxes?

1 2 3 4 5 6 7 8 9 10

Write over the number in the box.

How many seagulls can you count?

How many people can you see?

colour in Cranky the Crane.

Let's get counting

Stephen and Bridget are helping to brighten up the station! Can you help them to finish colouring in the picture of Percy?

THE FFARQUHAR QUARRY

1 Who is going over the bridge?

Bertie

2 Can you **find** these things in the big picture? Tick the box when you find each one.

3 How many butterflies can you count?

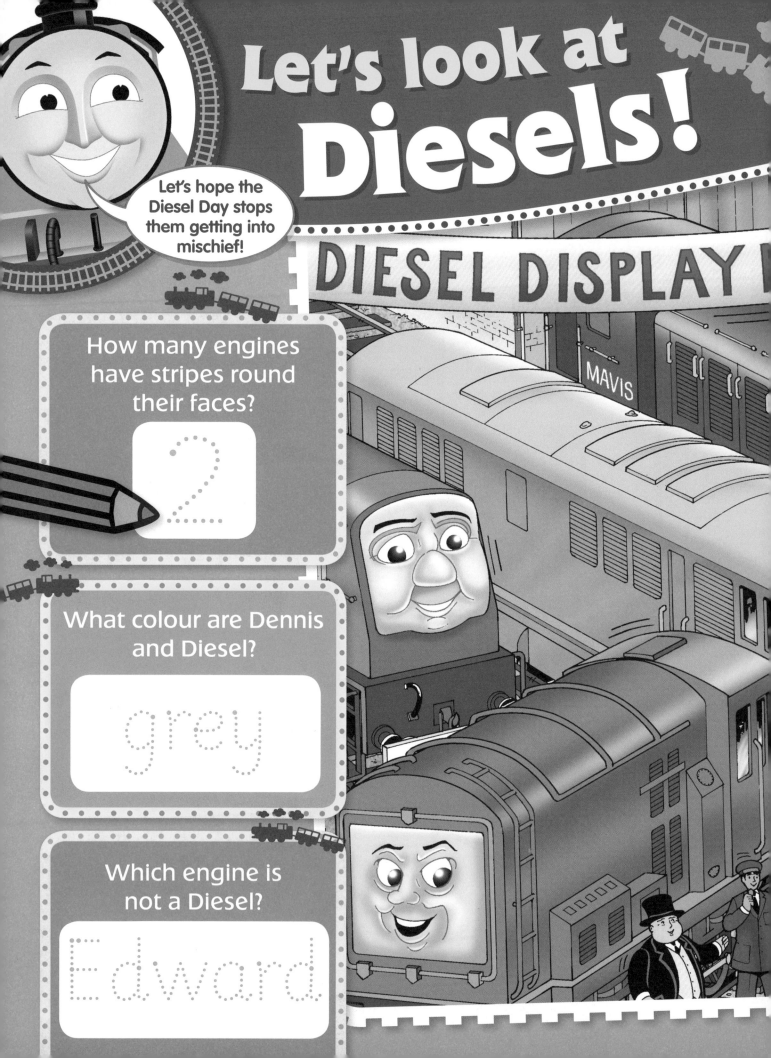

Let's look at Diesels!

Let's hope the Diesel Day stops them getting into mischief!

DIESEL DISPLAY

MAVIS

How many engines have stripes round their faces?

2

What colour are Dennis and Diesel?

grey

Which engine is not a Diesel?

Edward

The Diesels have been given a special day by The Fat Controller. Can you answer all these questions?

How many engines can you count on the page?

What is the name of the green engine in the middle of the picture?

BoCo

The Diesels need some fuel too. Draw over this drum of diesel oil and then pretend you are filling them up.

Let's repair
Can you count how many things there are in my way? There are quite a few!
BUS STOP
GEORGE

The Fat Controller's car is making funny sounds. Can you help him find the quickest way to the garage to get it repaired? Shout 'Beep! Beep!' when you get there.

GARAGE

Let's read!

Thomas helps Stephen and Bridget to see a guitar show!

A  group was arriving at the .

The  for their show had sold very quickly.  picked

up the  group and all their s from the . The

musicians thought  was a Really Useful Engine. Stephen

and Bridget wanted to go to the show but they didn't have any

. The Fat Controller asked  to take Stephen and

Bridget with him when he collected the  group to take

them back to the . When  picked up the

Special key

guitar Airport tickets Thomas

Read this story. When you get to a picture, guess the missing word. If you are stuck, use the special key at the bottom of the page.

group he told them that Stephen and

Bridget had not been able to get

any 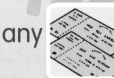 . The group

were so pleased with  ,

they sang songs and played

their s especially for the two children,

all the way to the . "I'm glad we didn't

get  !" said Bridget. "Thanks to

we've had our very own, special

 show," she laughed.

colour in this picture of Thomas.

Let's get puzzling!

This puzzle page is all about **music.**

1

Duncan is collecting a bell for the clock tower. Can you find the missing piece from this picture?

a

b

c

Use a pencil to practise writing the word.

bell

Peep! Peep! Toot! Toot!

2

Here are some colourful musical notes. Can you draw the next note in the pattern?

3

One of these musical instruments is different. Draw a ring around the odd one out.

a

b

c

d

4

Draw some strings on the guitar, then answer the question below.

Is this sentence true or false? Tick the box you think is right.

To play a guitar you use two drumsticks.

True ☐

False ☐

Let's practise writing

Terence the Tractor has been ploughing the fields but he's gone a bit off track!

Practise your writing by going over the lines Terence has made.

Let's Colour

Cranky has put a crate on the track to teach lazy Diesel a lesson. Add some colour to the picture.

CRANKY

Finish colouring in the crates.

How many green crates are there?

Practise drawing Billy's face by following each of the four steps. Then try drawing him on your own!

1

Draw two circles for eyes then two smaller circles inside for pupils.

2

Draw a curvy nose and two long wedge-shaped black eyebrows.

3

Draw a wide smile and some big white teeth that stick out.

4

Draw two full cheek lines and a shallow curve for his chin.

Let's make patterns

Look at these patterns and then count the circles in each row.
Write the number in the box.

Let's find out

Who can you see peeping out from behind the bushes?
Write the characters' names in the boxes.

Let's write

Write over these letters and words.

○○○○ ○○○○ ★ orange ★ owl

llll ★ orry ★ letters ○

ssss ★ saw stars

Draw over the dotty lines with your favourite pencils!

Let's count

Do the sums below and write over the number in the box to reveal the answer.

= 5

+ = 4

I hope that was trainloads of fun!

+ =

Henry is a big, strong engine. He can't puff along as quickly as Gordon but he pulls big loads and is Really Useful!

4

Now colour in the bushes with as many shades of **green** as you can find.

3

3

Let's look at Guards!

Guards on Sodor wear a blue uniform like me!

NAPFORD

2   K

5

Can you spot the **Guard** in this busy picture?

Circle the things a **Guard** needs to do his job.

Guards also check the tickets on the trains.

Guards make sure the trains run on time. Do these activities all about their job.

Counting Corner

How many passengers are in the picture?

PFORD

1 KNAPFO

Where is this ticket for?

Peel

Colour this **Guard** and draw a **green** flag for him to hold.

Look at the picture below.
Can you answer the questions
in the boxes?

Let's look and find!

Can you **find** these things in the big picture? Tick the box when you find each one.

Let's make a movie

How many people are in the film crew?

There is a film crew down at the Yard and all the engines are putting on their best show for them!

Who are the crew filming first?

Percy

What is in Gordon's truck?

What do you think happens next?
Draw some more of the coal that has spilled on to the track.

Let's Sort it out!

Toby gets in a spot of bother but I save the day!

1

But it was too late. Toby was left hanging over the edge of the river.

2

Luckily, Mavis was nearby and she pulled Toby to safety. "Thank you!" said Toby.

These pictures are out of order. Read the story and then write the order they should go in below.

3

One day, a Troublesome Truck gave Toby a mighty push.

4

"Stop it!" he cried. "I'm heading towards a rickety old bridge!"

The right order is:

Let's read!

Lady Hatt gets decorating in this story!

One day  visited the Main Station. "The Waiting Room needs a new coat of !" she told her husband.  decided to make it look nice for the . She asked  to pick up some .  steamed off to Knapford to pick up the . When she came back  was waiting for her so she could give the  to the decorator. The  was a lovely green colour, just like . When the painting was done,  found some curtains and comfy chairs to finish it off. The  were delighted. The next day  came back to the Main

Special key

 Lady Hatt    paint    passengers    Emily

Read this story. When you get to a picture, guess the missing word. If you are stuck, use the special key at the bottom of the page.

Station with her carriages but there

were no waiting. "Where

are all my ?"

wondered a puzzled .

Her driver went to search

for them. They were

all in the Waiting Room sitting in the comfy

chairs! " has made the Waiting Room

so nice the don't want to wait, they

want to stay. We'd better call it the

Sitting Room!" laughed .

Colour in this picture of Emily.

Let's get puzzling!

This puzzle page is all about the sights of Sodor!

1 Thomas is taking passengers for a special castle tour. Can you find the missing piece from this picture?

a

b

c

How many turrets can you see on the castle?

three

2 Henry is taking passengers to the countryside for a nature walk. Which route should he take?

1
2
3

3 Cranky is working hard at the Docks. Look at the picture then answer the questions.

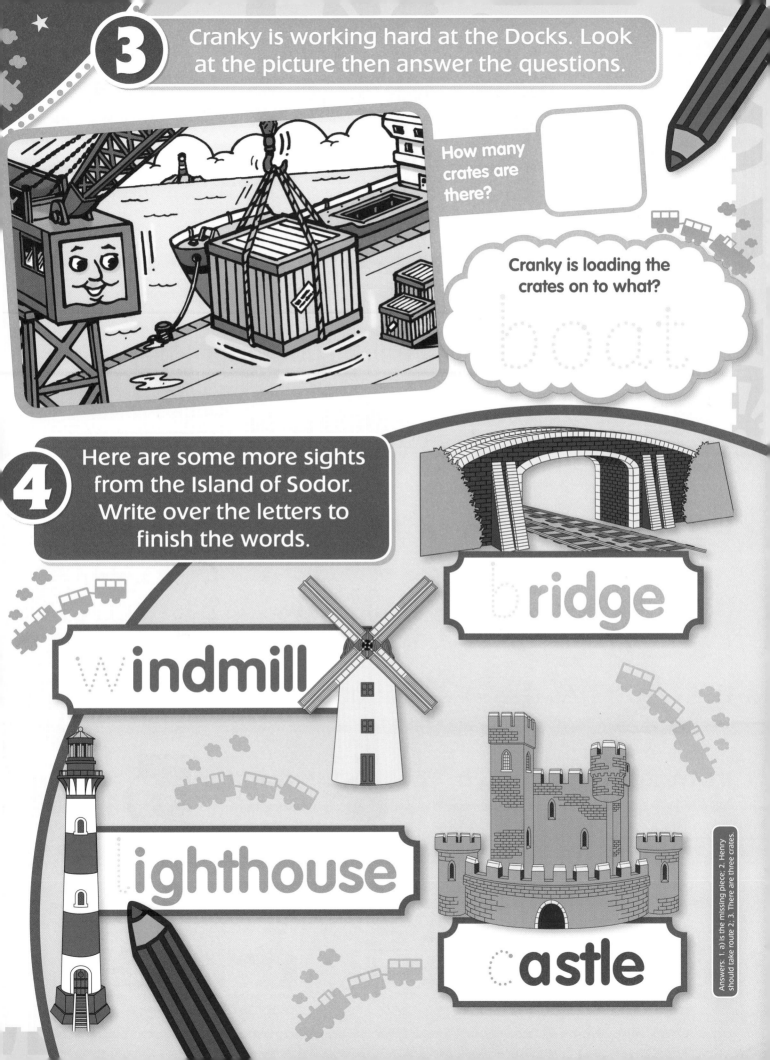

How many crates are there?

Cranky is loading the crates on to what?

boat

4 Here are some more sights from the Island of Sodor. Write over the letters to finish the words.

bridge

windmill

lighthouse

castle

Let's read!

Is it better to travel by boat or bus? Find out in this story!

"Bus trip around Sodor!" 's driver called. "Trips around the Bay!" shouted a  from a . Holidaymakers boarded the  and away it sailed, past the . "My trip would be just as good," sighed , "I could show the passengers the ." As the  chugged into Pebble Bay, its motor broke down. The  rang for  who kindly arrived to take the stranded holidaymakers back

Special key

Bertie   boat   Captain   lighthouse

Read this story. When you get to a picture, guess the missing word. If you are stuck, use the special key at the bottom of the page.

to the pier. "Travelling on is so

interesting!" said the holidaymakers.

When the was mended, they

couldn't decide whether to continue

their trip on  or by .

had an idea. He spoke to the  who

agreed and began to call, "Roll up for

a special trip by and bus!"

"An island tour by land AND sea is

twice as nice!" smiled .

Colour in this picture of Bertie.

Poor Henry has come off the track near the Quarry so a quarry crane is putting him back on the rails. **Colour** in the picture.

It's a lovely spring day and the diesels are spotting all the plants and animals that have appeared! Can you spot them too?

③ Can you **find** these things in the big picture? Tick the box when you find each one.

MAVIS

THE FFARQUHAR QUARRY CO. LTD.

Follow Jeremy's journey with a pencil as he loops and swoops through the sky.

How many birds are there?

What has Jeremy seen?

birds

Coming in to land!

Let's read!

Stephen has a lucky coin in this story!

 was taking  with Stephen and Bridget to a big house in the country. In the garden was a wishing well. "Drop a  in the wishing well and make a wish," smiled . "Then it might come true!" She opened her  and gave her grandchildren a  each. "I hope this  will bring me luck, " said Stephen. Later,  took everyone home again. But  suddenly had a shock. "I've lost my !" she cried. "Oh, no!" gasped Stephen. "My wish didn't work. It can't have been a lucky ! I didn't want Grandma's  to go

Special key

Thomas   Lady Hatt   coin   purse

Read this story. When you get to a picture, guess the missing word. If you are stuck, use the special key at the bottom of the page.

missing." Shortly, The Fat Controller

returned from work. "Look

what the cleaner

found on ,"

he said. It was 's missing 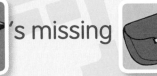. "It

had dropped down beside the seat!" he went

on. was delighted. So was Stephen.

"Something good did happen," he laughed.

"So maybe your 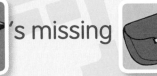 was lucky

after all!" chuckled .

Colour in this picture of Stephen.

Let's get puzzling!

This puzzle page is all about spring!

1 The trees are growing and Thomas is smiling. It must be spring again! Which piece is missing from this picture?

a

b

c

What is Thomas pulling?

trucks

2 Circle the two things you might see in springtime.

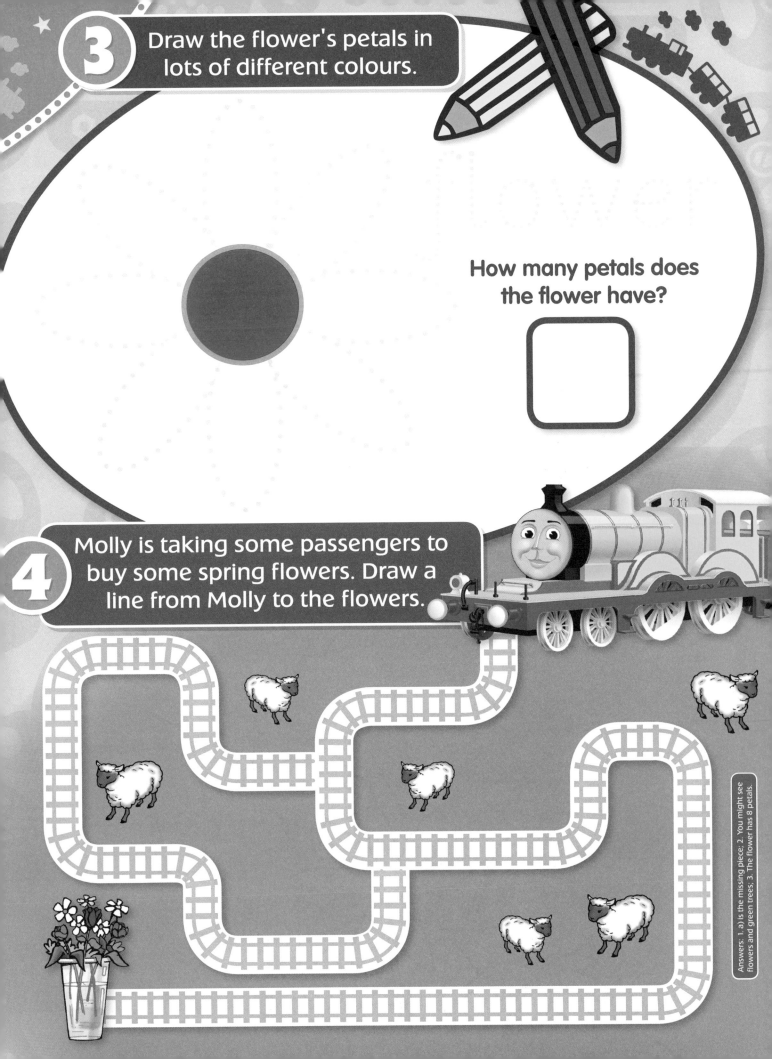

3 Draw the flower's petals in lots of different colours.

How many petals does the flower have?

4 Molly is taking some passengers to buy some spring flowers. Draw a line from Molly to the flowers.

Let's spot the difference

Write over a number when you spot a difference!

1 2

4 5

Answers: 1. Emily's body has turned yellow; 2. The boy with the watch is wearing a cap; 3. Edward's black pipe has disappeared; 4. The Fat Controller's tie is missing; 5. A guard is wearing a red jacket.

Thomas and James are both steam engines but they are different in lots of ways. See if you can tell some of the differences.

Thomas is

blue

1 Thomas has six red boiler bands.

2 He is engine number 1.

3 He has round portholes.

Draw a picture of you and your friend showing how different you are.

Are you taller or shorter?

Those Troublesome Trucks have been rocking and rolling again and now they have slipped off the track! "What a mess!" says The Fat Controller angrily.

3 Can you **find** these things in the big picture? Tick the box when you find each one.

Let's Visit the Harbour!

Trace and cut out Salty and take him round the track.

Salty has arrived at the Harbour. Take him for a trip to see his friends and pick up some loads on the way.

HARVEY

CRANKY

BULSTRODE

OIL

OIL

How many things does Salty pick up on the way round?

OIL

☐ + ☐ + ☐ = ☐

Let's clean Percy!

Can you help make me shiny and sparkling?

SWOOSH! SWOOSH!

1 Pour the water over Percy. **SWOOSH!** goes the water.

2 Spray some polish on Percy. **PSSSH!** goes the polish.

PSSSH! PSSSH!

Percy needs a good clean so he looks smart for a special job. Draw over the objects and make the sounds to help him scrub up!

3

Clean Percy with the cloth. **SQUEAK!** goes the cloth.

SQUEAK!

SQUEAK!

A strange squeak is a real mystery!

Let's read!

 was waiting outside Tidmouth Sheds while his

Fireman squirted  on his s so he would run smoothly.

" had a squeaky  yesterday," he said to the Driver.

"We're all steamed up and ready to go," replied 's Driver as

the fireman put down the  can and wiped his hands with a

rag. "Not quite," called . "Where's my Guard?" Just then

 and his crew heard a squeaking noise. "Smoke and steam!"

gasped . "I must need some more !" The squeaking

grew louder.  saw his Guard arriving on his . "Sorry I'm

Special key

 Duck    wheel    oil    bicycle

Read this story. When you get to a picture, guess the missing word. If you are stuck, use the special key at the bottom of the page.

late!" he called. "My

had a puncture so I had to

mend it!" "I think it needs

some too," grinned

the Fireman, fetching his

 can and rag. "We've

solved the riddle of the

mystery squeak," pipped

. "It is a  but a

 not a !"

Colour in this picture of Duck.

Let's get puzzling!

This puzzle page is all about the colour green!

1

Green engine Percy is shunting trucks for The Fat Controller. Which piece is missing from this picture?

a

b

c

How many people are in the picture?

three

2

Circle the objects that shouldn't be green.

3 Circle the green engine. Do you know his name?

I'm blue like Thomas!

There are ☐ engines.

4 Help Percy collect the green letters on his way to the mail room.

Dear Thomas and Friends
The Engine Sheds
The Island of Sodor
SD2 4TT

Mail Room

Percy collected ☐ green letters.

Let's join the dots!

The Fat Controller is flying high in a hot air balloon! Finish colouring the picture with your **pens or pencils!**

Which colours did you use?

Let's spot the difference

Can you spot the 5 differences in the bottom picture?

Write over a number when you spot a difference!

1

3 2

4 5

Rosie

When Rosie first came to Sodor, she copied everything Thomas did. This annoyed him a lot.

Rosie helped Thomas more than once and now Thomas and Rosie are very good friends.

Rosie is one of the few lucky engines to have coloured wheels. Her wheels are bright red!

Let's colour

Thomas and his passengers have been caught in a spring shower. Use your crayons to add some colour to the picture.

Look at the picture below. Can you answer the questions

1 2 3 4 5 6 7 8 9 10

How many pairs of wellies can you see?

How many cows are in the field?

Write over the number in the box.

4

How many adults are holding umbrellas?

Answers: There are 5 umbrellas, 3 cows, 7 pairs of wellies and 2 adults holding umbrellas.

Let's help

Help The Fat Controller get to the Engine Shed to check on his sleeping engines.

Whisper the names of the three sleeping engines.